Sleep Tight, Anna Banana!

By Dominique Roques

Illustrated by Alexis Dormal

:01

First Second

New York

It's late at night. Anna Banana is still reading, even though her parents said, "Lights out!"

But her book is fascinating...

...frightening...

...hilarious...

...gripping!

Ha! Ha! Ha!

You laugh too loud. I'm going to sleep somewhere else.

But Anna likes to have ALL her stuffed animals around her.

Fuzzball tries to turn off the light.

Nope.

Then Zigzag sings a lullaby to make Anna sleepy.

Not happening.

Pingpong makes a dash for it.

Not a chance!

Nothing works.

Finally, Anna yawns.

She arranges her stuffed animals around her pillow...

...and slips under her comforter.

Click.

Good night, Whaley!

And me?

Good night, Fuzzball!

And they all fall sound asleep.

First Second

Ana Ana - *Douce nuit* © DARGAUD 2012 by Alexis Dormal & Dominique Roques
All rights reserved – www.dargaud.com

Lettering by Marion Vitus
English translation by Mark Siegel
English translation copyright © 2014 by First Second

Published by First Second
First Second is an imprint of Roaring Brook Press, a division of Holtzbrinck Publishing Holdings Limited Partnership
175 Fifth Avenue, New York, New York 10010
All rights reserved

Cataloging-in-Publication Data is on file at the Library of Congress

ISBN: 978-1-62672-019-0

First Second books may be purchased for business or promotional use. For information on bulk purchases please contact Macmillan Corporate and Premium Sales Department at (800) 221-7945 x5442 or by email at specialmarkets@macmillan.com.

Originally published in France by Dargaud as *Ana Ana: Douce nuit.*
First American edition 2014
Book design by Colleen AF Venable

Printed in China by South China Printing Co. Ltd., Dongguan City, Guangdong Province
10 9 8 7 6 5 4 3 2 1